William's Gift

Story created by Liz Farrington
Written by Jennifer C. Weil
Illustrated by Hui Han Liu

Enchanté Publishing

William spotted the perfect place on the Christmas tree to hang his clear glass icicle. Standing on his toes, he reached high and— the icicle slipped through his fingers. William closed his eyes and held his breath, hoping it wouldn't break. Plink! The icicle shattered on the floor.

"You're so clumsy!" his brother Jackson said.

"What a klutz!" said his sister Lenore.

"William, that's the second thing you've messed up. You already twisted the tinsel so it can't be used, and now this." His father's voice sounded tired and angry. "If you can't be careful, go sit on the sofa and be still."

"But, Dad—"

"Don't 'but Dad' me," Dad cut in. "Just sit. Stay there until you calm down."

William's Gift

Enchanté books are dedicated to the children who inspired them

Series concept by Ayman Sawaf and Kevin Ryerson
Developed from true stories by Liz Farrington
Copyright ©1994 by Enchanté Publishing
MRS. MURGATROYD character copyright ©1993 by Enchanté
MRS. MURGATROYD is a trademark of Enchanté
Series format and design by Jaclyne Scardova

Enchanté Publishing
120 Hawthorne, Palo Alto, CA 94301

Printed in Singapore

ISBN 1-56844-007-3

First Edition
10 9 8 7 6 5 4 3 2 1

What lies at the end of the rainbow? Is there merely a pot of gold, or might there be another sort of treasure — a treasure that may be reached by anyone willing to undertake the journey?

For if you follow the rainbow to its end and look into its shimmering colors, you will find a great oak tree with a door at the base of the trunk.

If you open the door and step inside, you will meet Mrs. Murgatroyd, the wise woman who lives there. In her paint pots she collects all the colors of the rainbow.

And if you take up a paintbrush and picture whatever is in your heart, you will discover a treasure far more valuable than gold.

Sitting stiffly on the sofa, William heard his family's harsh words again in his mind. He scrunched up his face to hold back the tears. *It's not fair*, he thought. *I tried to do it right. They said I could help and now they won't let me!*

He picked at a hole in the seam of the sofa cushion and began to pull out clumps of stuffing. Slowly, the pile of stuffing grew into a small mountain.

Jackson glanced up from the new box of tinsel he was opening. "Oh, man, look at what Willie's doing!" he said.

"Dad!" Lenore shrieked.

"William, go to your room. Now!" said Dad. "And stay there until your mother gets home from work."

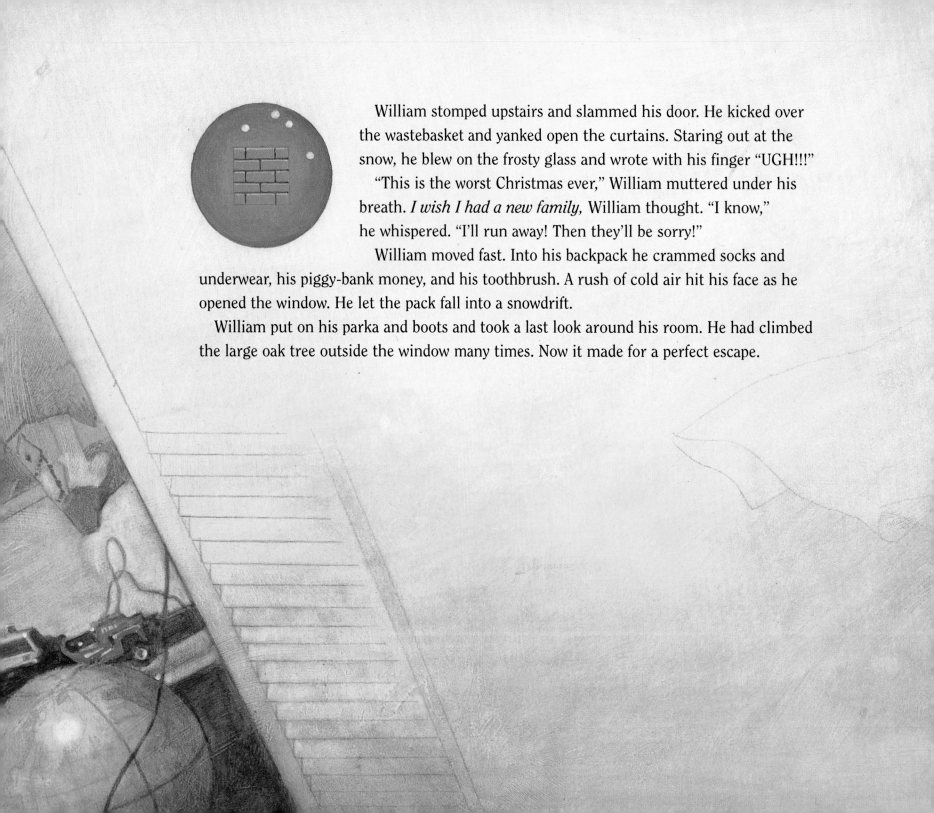

William stomped upstairs and slammed his door. He kicked over the wastebasket and yanked open the curtains. Staring out at the snow, he blew on the frosty glass and wrote with his finger "UGH!!!"

"This is the worst Christmas ever," William muttered under his breath. *I wish I had a new family,* William thought. "I know," he whispered. "I'll run away! Then they'll be sorry!"

William moved fast. Into his backpack he crammed socks and underwear, his piggy-bank money, and his toothbrush. A rush of cold air hit his face as he opened the window. He let the pack fall into a snowdrift.

William put on his parka and boots and took a last look around his room. He had climbed the large oak tree outside the window many times. Now it made for a perfect escape.

At the bottom, William struggled to get his pack on over his parka. The wind was cold on his face and it hurt his throat to breathe the icy air.

William inched his way around the house. When he reached the living room window, he peered in. The room was empty now except for the tree. All the lights were aglow, and under the tree were colorful packages tied with shiny ribbons.

William wondered whether he had gotten *Alpha Run*, the computer game he wanted so much. He hesitated, feeling sad and unsure about running away. Then he remembered his family's mean words and his anger came back. He turned away to leave.

William's feet, even in his hiking boots, felt cold. He kept his hands in his pockets, but without gloves they were soon red and painful from the cold. "What a dummy I was to forget gloves. Clumsy and dumb!"

He could tell it was getting later as the sun sank lower in the sky. William passed house after brightly decorated house. *I bet everybody's happy but me*, he thought glumly.

The huge tree in the window of one inviting house caught William's eye. Its twinkling lights and glass ornaments sparkled like rainbows, reminding him of a happy place he had visited once in a dream. William stamped his feet to shake off some of the wet snow on his boots. His feet were so cold he felt like they were frozen in blocks of ice.

All at once, the snow-covered path glittered with color. William blinked and rubbed his eyes, but the colors did not go away. He looked up and saw a smiling woman framed in the light pouring through the open door of a hollow tree. She looked like the woman in his dream.

"Hello, William," she said. "You're out late."

"Mrs. Murgatroyd?"

"You must be freezing. Come inside."

In no time, Mrs. Murgatroyd had settled William in front of a toasty fire. She pulled off his boots and wrapped a big quilt around him. She poured warm water from the kettle into a tub so he could soak his feet. She rubbed his cold hands between her warm ones. As he began to thaw out, William felt the feeling return to his feet as a tingling sensation. The tingling was a little painful and reminded him of the time his foot fell asleep in class and he tried to walk on it.

Nestled in the sleepy warmth of the room, under Mrs. Murgatroyd's comforting care, William began to feel better. Christmas and his family seemed far away. He looked around and his eyes were drawn to a shelf where the rainbow colors flowed into paint pots. William felt calm just watching them.

"I see you've noticed my magical paints." Smiling, Mrs. Murgatroyd placed fresh paper, brushes, and pots of paint on a table near the fire. "Help yourself," she said.

William liked to paint, but he hid most of his pictures because Jackson and Lenore made fun of them. Suddenly, all the mean things they said that afternoon came rushing back to him, and his feelings were hurt all over again. William sighed. *I don't like feeling this way,* he thought.

William picked up a brush and dipped it into a pot of green paint. As if it had a mind of its own, the brush moved quickly across the paper. A huge Christmas tree appeared. *I didn't mean to paint that!* William thought. But instead of stopping, he decorated it with colorful ornaments, a gold star, and lots of lights. Beneath the tree, he painted piles of presents.

"Now for a Santa's helper." William added an elf, then sat back and studied his work. "I'll make it a computer game!" he said with delight. "Jackson hardly ever lets me play with his game, but I can play with this one all I want!"

William asked Mrs. Murgatroyd for more paper, then outlined a control panel and a joy stick. He painted buttons for freezing the action and for speeding it up. He labeled the two biggest buttons POWER ON and POWER OFF.

William was having fun creating his game. "The goal is for Elf to decorate the tree before the Meanies can stop him," William said, "and it won't be easy! Elf has to find all the decorations hidden in the living room and carry them through SAFE PASSAGE—that door on the right. He has to take chances like balancing on the back of the sofa and creeping along the edges of the bookshelves. And he has to stay away from the Meanies!"

William touched POWER ON. The screen lit up and BEGIN GAME flashed at the bottom. "Oh, wow!" William hollered.

Joy stick in hand, he moved Elf across the fireplace mantel. Hidden behind the vase was the bright gold star Elf needed to freeze the Meanies so he could continue on his journey.

As Elf reached for the star, a Meanie that looked like Lenore jumped out from behind a picture frame. "You'll never make it," she said.

William hesitated. DON'T LET OTHER PEOPLE'S WORDS BOTHER YOU flashed at the bottom of the screen.

"Right on!" William said. He took a breath, then calmly placed Elf where he could grab the star and use it to freeze Meanie Lenore. "All right!" he said gleefully.

Next, Elf leaped to the bookcase, where he found seven ornaments stashed behind the books. As he put the last treasure into his sack, he slipped off the shelf and plunged to the bottom of the screen.

Meanie Lenore unfroze and began to laugh. Two Meanies who looked like Jackson and Dad laughed, too. GAME OVER flashed on the screen.

William felt clumsy and stupid, but he remembered the computer's advice: DON'T LET OTHER PEOPLE'S WORDS BOTHER YOU. He pushed BEGIN GAME and led Elf halfway to SAFE PASSAGE before Meanie Dad popped out from under a pillow and scared him. Elf dropped his sack of ornaments, but William did not give up. Once more he pushed BEGIN GAME and this time Elf made it all the way to SAFE PASSAGE.

"Ha!" William said. "I'm not clumsy or stupid—If I just take time to think about it first, I can do it!"

Through SAFE PASSAGE lay the cold, snowy world of Level Two. CHOOSE YOUR BURDENS flashed on the screen. William picked HURT FEELINGS, BLAME, FEELING SORRY FOR YOURSELF, ANGER, and FEELING CLUMSY. Elf had to pack each burden into a snowball and throw it into the trash pile where it belonged. If he didn't get rid of them, the burdens would slow him down and he would freeze before he could get back to the safety of HOME.

William started with HURT FEELINGS. Elf threw it as hard as he could. Up jumped an Abominable Snowman and batted it back. No matter how fast Elf threw or where he aimed, the Snowman sent the burden flying back to him.

"I can't do anything right!" William shouted. Frustrated, he turned to Mrs. Murgatroyd. She pointed to one of the buttons on the panel. William hit the PAUSE button to stop the action and calm down. After he thought for a moment, William went on with the game.

He had Elf pretend to throw. This time when the Snowman jumped up, Elf threw the burden past him and straight into the pile of trash.

Now that he knew how to outwit the Snowman, Elf quickly threw all his burdens into the trash.

"Yes!" William cheered.

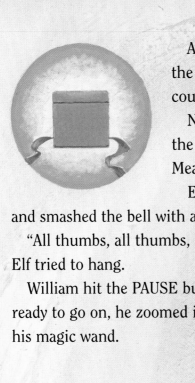

At the bottom of the screen, along with a dozen pictures, flashed the words ACCEPT YOUR GIFT. William chose a magic wand that could change hurtful words or actions into helpful ones.

Now Elf had reached Level Three of the game. It was time to trim the tree. The pace picked up as Elf took an ornament out of his sack. Meanie Jackson flicked it away, shouting "Bumble fingers!"

Elf began to hang a glass bell when suddenly, Meanie Dad appeared and smashed the bell with a hammer. "What makes you think you can trim a tree?" he asked.

"All thumbs, all thumbs, all thumbs down!" Meanie Lenore chanted, shattering the angel Elf tried to hang.

William hit the PAUSE button to freeze the action and took a deep breath. When he felt ready to go on, he zoomed in on the Meanies. Elf tapped each one lightly on the forehead with his magic wand.

"You don't know how much you hurt my feelings," Elf said. "When you're mean to me, first I want to disappear, then I want to hurt you back. But that won't fix things."

The Meanies unfroze one by one, their frowns turning to smiles. "This is a big tree and if we all work together, we can make it the most beautiful Christmas tree ever," they said as they helped Elf decorate the tree. When it sparkled with lights and ornaments, Elf leaped high into the air and placed his gold star at the very top of the tree.

GAME OVER, WELL DONE! flashed three times. Then the screen went dark.

"Game over, well done," William repeated. He had helped Elf reach his goal, through all the challenges, and guided his every move. Even the Meanies had listened. William felt able and smart and strong.

All at once William wanted to go home. He gathered his things, thanked Mrs. Murgatroyd, and hurried on his way.

William's good feelings warmed him all the way home. He knew just what to say to his family. He might be a bit clumsy, but he knew that he *could* do some things, and that was cool.

When he reached his house, William looked through the living room window. *I'm not too late!* he thought. There were still decorations to hang on the tree, and presents to give and to receive. William smiled at his reflection in the glass.

Inside, he went straight to the Christmas tree. Beneath it was a present with his name on it. He picked it up. The weight and size were right. So was the shape.

"It's *Alpha Run!*" he hollered. "Merry Christmas to me!"

When they heard his voice, Dad, Lenore, and Jackson came running. "Where were you? Are you okay?" they asked with concern.

Through the window, William could see the bright colors of the lights sparkling on the snow. William smiled. Then he picked up the shiny gold star, climbed the stepladder, and placed the most beautiful ornament of all at the top of the tree.